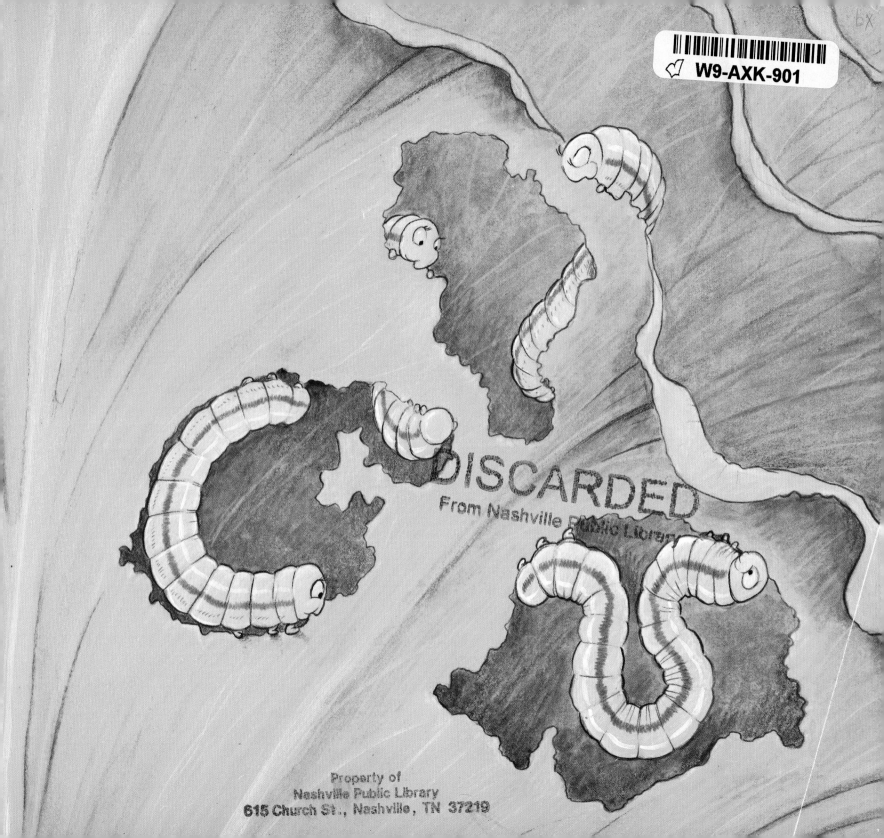

Clara Caterpillar

by Pamela Duncan Edwards • illustrated by Henry Cole

HarperCollins*Publishers*

One day a cream-colored butterfly laid an egg on a cabbage leaf.

"Grow up to be courageous and contented, Clara," she called to her egg as the wind carried her away.

Clara lay curled in the egg case for a considerable time. Eventually a crowd of caterpillars clustered around her.

"She's incredibly late coming out," commented one.

"She's very cautious," agreed another.

A curious caterpillar knocked
on Clara's egg case.
"This is Cornelius," he said.
"Come on out!"
"But I'm comfortable
in here," called Clara.

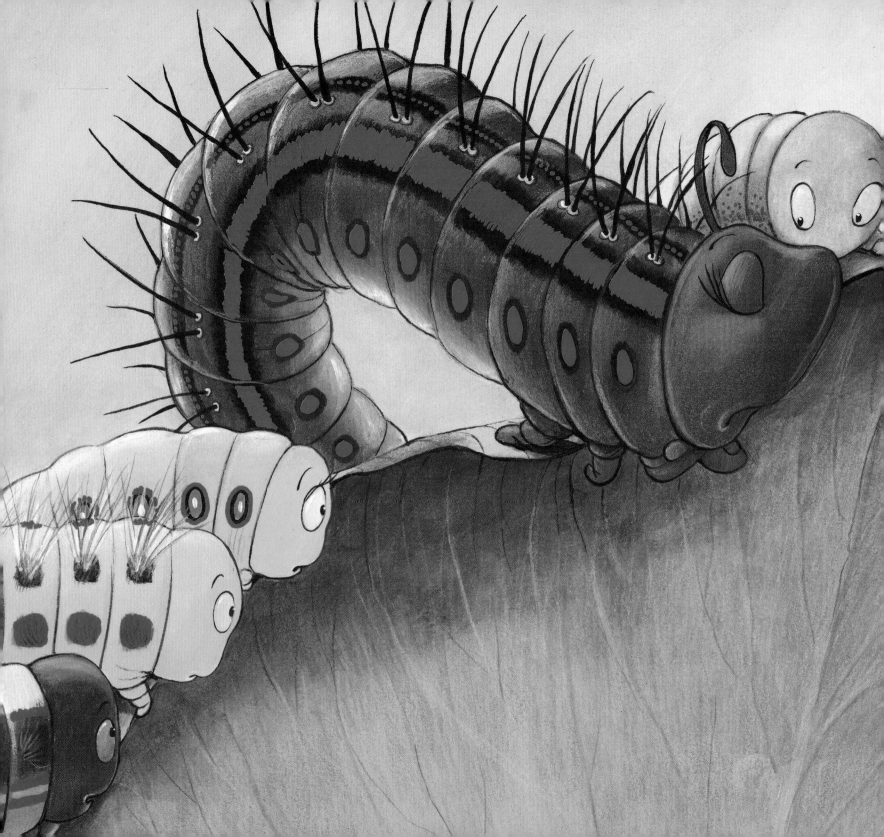

"Who cares if she comes out?" scoffed a scowling caterpillar called Catisha. "It's clear she'll only be a cabbage caterpillar. Cabbage caterpillars are so common."

"Don't be cruel, Catisha," Cornelius scolded. "Cabbage caterpillars are cute."

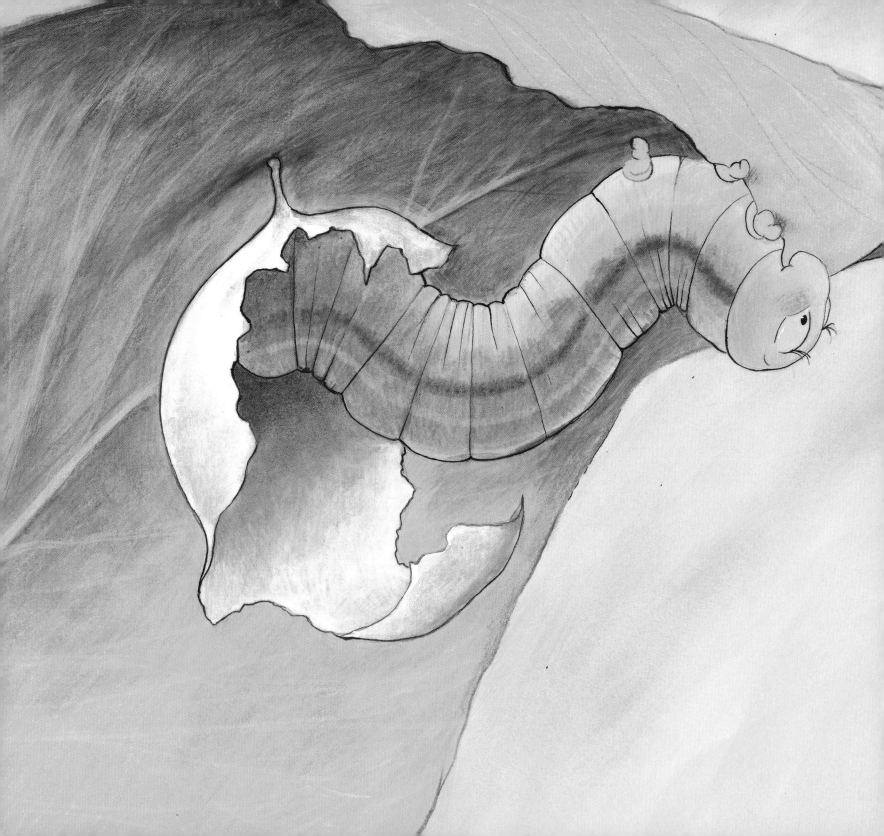

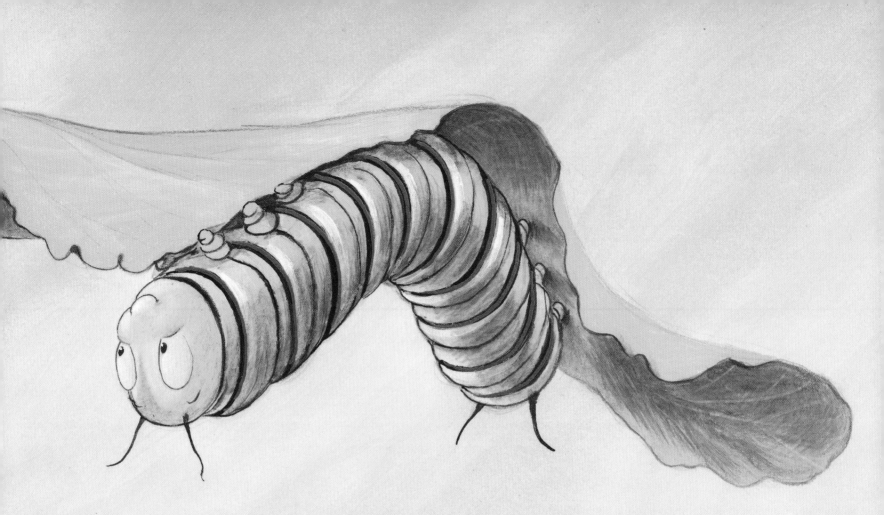

"Did you say cabbage?" cried Clara. "Cabbage sounds scrumptious!" So Clara cut a hole in her egg case and clambered out.

"I'm a lucky caterpillar," she said. "Cornelius! Come and share this delectable cabbage!"

Clara and Cornelius climbed and crawled and capered about. They had carefree caterpillar fun.

They crammed themselves with cabbage, carrot, and cauliflower leaves.

They grew into colossal caterpillars.

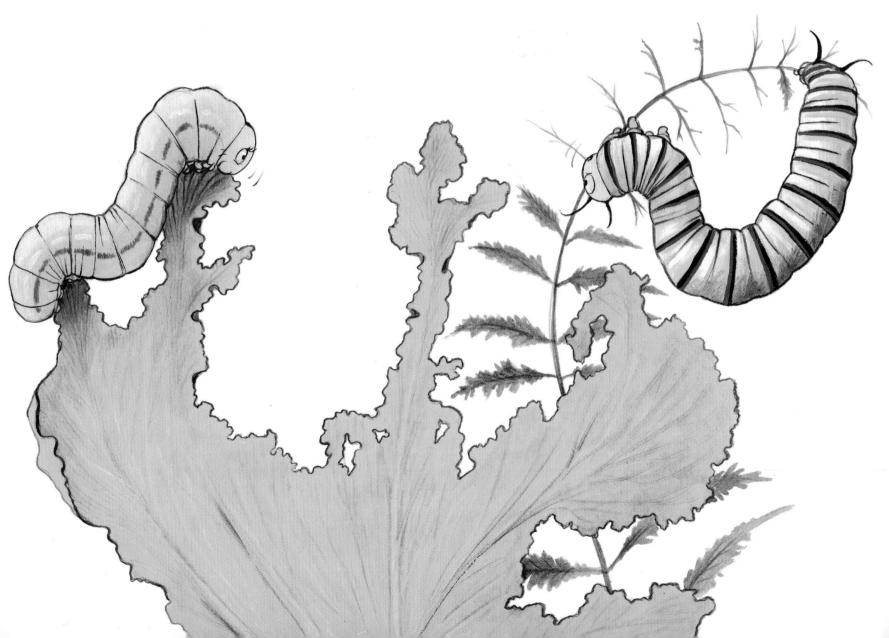

Then one day
Cornelius called, "Clara,
come and make your chrysalis."
    "Don't encourage her," mocked Catisha.
"She's only going to become a common cabbage
butterfly."

"Why is Catisha
being catty?" Clara asked.
"Catisha is conceited," comforted Cornelius.
"She knows she'll become an attractive
crimson-colored butterfly."

Then Clara, Cornelius, and the other
caterpillars caught on to the cabbage,
carrot, and cauliflower plants
with cottony threads.

They crinkled and discarded their skins
and cuddled down inside their chrysalises.

"Coo-ey!" cried Cornelius to Clara. "Are you comfortable?"

"Actually, I'm very cozy," Clara called back.

Then, one morning, the chrysalises began to crack, and out climbed delicate creatures.

"Coooool!" cried Clara. "You all look captivating! Cornelius, you're a terrific copper color!"

"Why is that scruffy creature conversing with us?" complained a scowling crimson-colored butterfly.

"Catisha!" Clara said. "You are SPECTACULAR!"

"Of course," replied Catisha.
"And you, Clara, are so CREAM!"
"I think cream is cute," declared Cornelius.
"Cute!" Catisha snickered. "Don't be ridiculous, Cornelius!"

Then Catisha climbed toward the clouds on her scaly cobweb wings.

Suddenly a crow cawed and scared everyone. "Snacktime!" he exclaimed as he caught sight of the crimson-colored Catisha. The butterflies panicked and frantically scattered in all directions.

"You can't escape!" screeched the crow to Catisha.

"Catisha! I'm coming to the rescue!" cried Clara.

"Clara, be careful," screamed Cornelius.

Plucking up her courage, Clara flicked her wings at the crow.

"Catch me if you can, you scalawag!" she taunted.

Then Clara curved down and ducked into a camellia bush.

The crow became confused and forgot about
Catisha. He cocked his head and pecked in the
petals. But Clara, the cream-colored butterfly,
lay camouflaged behind a curtain of
cream-colored camellias.

"That's curious," complained
the crestfallen crow. "I was confident
I could capture a succulent snack."

"The coast is clear!" Cornelius shouted. "The crisis is over!"

"Congratulations, Clara," complimented the other butterflies.

"Clara, you're so clever," cried the shocked Catisha. "I could never camouflage myself like you. I'm too colorful. I was crazy to scoff at your cream color. It's incredible."

"And cute, too!" declared Cornelius.

Cornelius clapped his wings.
"Listen carefully," he commanded. "That crow is
a scoundrel! Let's cling close to Clara. Clara can stop
him from catching us. Clara is so capable and courageous."
"Clara is lucky to be cream colored," said Catisha.

"And I'm a completely contented butterfly," said Clara.

To sweet Alex—
may you grow up to be
courageous and contented

—P.D.E.

For Marion, whose appreciation
and respect for nature
has always been an inspiration to me

—H.C.

Clara Caterpillar
Text copyright © 2001 by Pamela Duncan Edwards
Illustrations copyright © 2001 by Henry Cole
Printed in the U.S.A. All rights reserved.
www.harperchildrens.com

Library of Congress Cataloging-in-Publication Data
Edwards, Pamela Duncan.
     Clara Caterpillar / by Pamela Duncan Edwards ; illustrated by Henry Cole.
         p.   cm.
     Summary: By camouflaging herself, Clara Caterpillar, who becomes a cream-colored butterfly,
courageously saves Catisha the crimson-colored butterfly from a hungry crow.
     ISBN 0-06-028995-3 — ISBN 0-06-028996-1 (lib. bdg.)
     [1. Butterflies—Fiction.   2. Metamorphosis—Fiction.]   I. Cole, Henry, date, ill.   II. Title.
PZ7.E26365 Cl   2001   00-32010
[E]—dc21   CIP
                                                                                                              AC

Typography by Elynn Cohen   1   2   3   4   5   6   7   8   9   10   ❖   First Edition